For Katie, a knight in
shining armour – M.S.

For Theodore
and Nancy – E.E.

BLOOMSBURY CHILDREN'S BOOKS
Bloomsbury Publishing Plc
50 Bedford Square, London, WC1B 3DP, UK

BLOOMSBURY, BLOOMSBURY CHILDREN'S BOOKS and the Diana logo are trademarks of Bloomsbury Publishing Plc

First published in Great Britain 2018 by Bloomsbury Publishing Plc

Text copyright © Mark Sperring 2018
Illustration copyright © Ed Eaves 2018

Mark Sperring and Ed Eaves have asserted their rights under the Copyright, Design and Patents Act, 1988,
to be identified as the Author and Illustrator of this work

A catalogue record for this book is available from the British Library

ISBN: HB: 978 1 4088 7398 4; PB: 978 1 4088 7399 1; eBook: 978 1 4088 7397 7

2 4 6 8 10 9 7 5 3 1

Printed in China by Leo Paper Products, Heshan, Guangdong

All papers used by Bloomsbury Publishing Plc are natural, recyclable products from
wood grown in well managed forests. The manufacturing processes conform to
the environmental regulations of the country of origin

To find out more about our authors and books visit www.bloomsbury.com and sign up for our newsletters

For my big brother Jonathan Farber
with love your little sister Suzi x x x ~ SM

For Alberto, thanks for making me laugh everyday.
And Olivia, Victoria and Andres, for your support,
you are all awesome! ~ ES

Bloomsbury Publishing, London, Oxford, New York, New Delhi and Sydney

First published in Great Britain in 2016 by Bloomsbury Publishing Plc
50 Bedford Square, London, WC1B 3DP

Text copyright © Suzi Moore 2016
Illustrations copyright © Erica Salcedo 2016
The moral rights of the author and illustrator have been asserted

A CIP catalogue record for this book is available from the British Library

ISBN 978 1 4088 4494 6 (HB)
ISBN 978 1 4088 4495 3 (PB)
ISBN 978 1 4088 4493 9 (eBook)

Printed in China by Leo Paper Products, Heshan, Guangdong

1 3 5 7 9 10 8 6 4 2

www.bloomsbury.com

All papers used by Bloomsbury Publishing are natural, recyclable products
made from wood grown in well-managed forests.
The manufacturing processes conform to the
environmental regulations of the country of origin

BLOOMSBURY is a registered trademark of Bloomsbury Publishing Plc

Wolfish
Stew

Suzi Moore

Erica Salcedo

BLOOMSBURY
LONDON OXFORD NEW YORK NEW DELHI SYDNEY

There once was a **rabbit** whose name was **Grey**. And he went to the woods to pick berries one day.

With a basket in hand he skipped along.
As he skipped down the path he sang this song:

"I must stick to the path, I must stay on the trail.
I must always look out for the

BIG BUSHY TAIL."

For deep in the woods lived a **wolf** called **Blue** who wanted little Grey for his **Wolfish** stew.

Blue was **cunning.**

He was **sneaky** and **mean.**

He had the
bushiest
tail
you've ever seen!

Watch out, Grey!
Be careful, please!

Oh no, Grey. Please watch out!
That's not a log!

It's a WOLFISH SNOUT!

"Take care, Grey!" the birds all tweet. "Could **that** be a **pair** of

WOLFISH FEET!"

EEK!

Stick to the **path**, Grey! **Stay** on the **trail**!
Remember to **look out** for the

BIG BUSHY...

Quick now,
Grey,

from stone

to stone.

Be Careful, Grey,

you're not alone!

A **WOLFISH** tail...

a **WOLFISH** snout...
Quick now, Grey!
Don't get caught out!

WOLFISH knees...

WOLFISH feet.

You're about to become a WOLFISH TREAT.

But **clever** little Grey, as quick as quick,
has thought of a clever little **rabbitty trick!**
So into the woods Blue runs on...
Until...

"Where's that Grey?
Where has he gone?"

wolf traps

Um...stay on the trail...
Always look out for the...

BIG BUSHY TAIL."

"Oh dear me!" little Grey said.
"Looks like you've been caught instead!"

"Into my **pot** and into my **brew**.
Now **that's** what I call a